LAZY JONES

SHEILA KELLY WELCH

illustrated by
Philip Webb

Learning Media

1.

RAIN!

I don't expect you to believe me, but I'm going to tell you what happened anyhow.

It had been raining for days and days. My sister Patty had dragged every puzzle down from the attic on the first day of the rain, but even she was getting bored now. "I wish it would stop so we could go outside and shoot some hoops," she said.

"Not me," I said.

"You are *so* lazy. Lazy Bones Jones, that's you!"

"My name is L.B. and don't forget it!" I snapped. Patty always calls me Lazy Bones when everyone *knows* that my real name is Laurence Bradley Jones. All my friends call me L.B., but my sister is *not* one of my friends.

"Are you going to help me with this puzzle or not … Lazy Bones?"

"Not," I frowned. "I'm not going to help you with that puzzle or any puzzle because you never let me put in the last piece."

"Why should you when I do most of the work?" she asked.

Just then, our dog galloped into the room. "Get away, Klutz!" screamed Patty. But Klutz crashed into her and her puzzle. Pieces flew everywhere. I laughed. Klutz wagged his tail. Thump! Thump!

"Go away!" Patty yelled as she picked up the puzzle. "Rain! Boys! Dogs!" she muttered. "You're all driving me nuts!"

I tried the TV, but there was nothing I wanted to watch. I was bored. No, I was beyond bored. Klutz came over to the couch and pushed his nose under my hand. I saw a tiny blue piece of Patty's puzzle sticking to the fur by his ear. I slipped it into my jeans pocket.

"This is such a cool puzzle," Patty said. "I wish I could be there instead of here." She'd done most of it already. I could see a waterfall, a pond, and a bunch of trees.

"Boring," I said.

"No, it's not. Use your imagination, Lazy Bones. I bet there's a unicorn hiding in the forest, *and* a castle up there on the mountain."

"Looks like a big hill to me," I said.

Patty ignored me. "Maybe there's a princess in the castle," she said.

"Boring! Who cares about a dumb princess?"

"You have no imagination, Lazy Bones." Then suddenly she yelled, "Oh, no! There's a piece missing!"

"Really?" I said. "That's a real shame." I leaned over to look, and sure enough, there was a hole in the middle of the boring blue pond.

Patty looked around on the floor for a few minutes. Then she said, "I'm going up into the attic to see if I can find it. Watch Klutz, OK?"

I nodded, smiling. As soon as she'd gone, I hopped up to look at the puzzle. Klutz came over to look, and his big nose bumped into my arm. "Careful, boy," I said. "You'll spoil my surprise." I took the missing piece from my pocket and lined up the edges with the hole. I could feel Klutz's hot breath on my hand. He was really getting into this. He rested his chin on the edge of the puzzle. I grinned as I pressed the tiny piece into place. Then –

POOF! SPLASH!

2. HELP!

ater!

I sank down into the darkness. I wanted to yell, but yelling underwater is not a good idea. And I can't swim either! My swimming teacher tells me to relax, but how can you relax when you know you're drowning? I pulled upwards with my arms and got to the surface. "Help!" I spluttered.

Just before I sank again, I saw something large and furry. A water monster? As I splashed around, the "thing" bumped against me, and I grabbed hold of it. I couldn't stop myself. Anything was better than drowning.

I felt myself being pulled through the water to the edge of the pond. I couldn't stop coughing, my eyes stung, and my ears were full of water. The monster came over and gave me a quick lick and shook water all over me. Then he whacked me with a stringy, "life-saving" tail. "Klutz, it's you!" I said. "Thanks, boy! You saved me."

I patted Klutz and squinted at the pond. It sparkled with bright sunlight. But this was very strange! Wasn't I just sitting in my own boring living room a minute ago? And what was that roaring sound? I shaded my eyes against the sun and saw the waterfall. I blinked and shook my head. "Klutz," I whispered, "Are you having the same dream as I am? Well, I guess the good thing about dreams is that you get to wake up."

I pinched my arm. I jumped up and down. Nothing, except the sound of water slooshing around in my ears. The waterfall and forest stayed there – just like in Patty's puzzle. Was my sister somewhere up there looking down? Could she see me? I found a stick and wrote in the sand, "It's me, L.B. Help!" Nothing happened.

I scrambled up onto one of the boulders and yelled, "Patty! Help!" But my words were drowned out by the sound of the waterfall. Klutz thought I was calling him and clawed his way up onto the boulder. He put his gigantic paws on my shoulders and tried to lick my face. We both fell backward onto the sandy ground. "Ouch!"

Now I was scared, and angry too. This was Patty's puzzle world. Why was I inside it? I pounded my fist into the sand. I felt Klutz's hot breath on the back of my neck. "Go away, silly dog!" More hot breath … and something sharp touching my back. "Klutz?" I said slowly. I heard a scared whimper, but the sound came from about ten feet away.

The sharp thing prodded me again. Then a fierce voice said, "Get up!" If Klutz could talk, he would say things like "Sit, boy! Come, boy!" But this voice sounded angry.

"Now, boy!" it boomed.

I stood up but my knees felt like wet noodles.

"Turn around," said the voice.

3.
UNICORN!

I didn't want to turn around,
but the voice was very powerful.
I couldn't help myself.
And there,
standing in front
of me was …
a unicorn!
I sputtered,
but no words
came out of
my mouth.

"Who are you?" the unicorn asked.

I gulped. "I'm L.B. Jones."

"What are you doing here?"

"I don't know. I was just doing nothing, and all of a sudden ... here I am."

"Doing nothing?" The unicorn had eyes like the ones Patty draws on horses.

"I was bored."

The unicorn blinked. "Bored?"

"Yes! And stop asking questions, would you? I don't know what happened!"

"Humans are not welcome here," the unicorn said with a toss of his head. His horn glinted in the sun.

I thought about asking him whether dogs were welcome, but Klutz was hiding behind a boulder, so I said, "If you want me to leave, you'll have to help me find my way home."

"Don't you have a plan?" he asked.

Plan? I had no plan. Plans take imagination, and as Patty always says, I have none.

Suddenly the unicorn lowered his head and charged behind the boulder. He caught Klutz under the collar and lifted him high into the air. "Stop! That's my dog!" I screamed.

The beast lowered his head and stepped backwards, sliding his horn out from the collar. Klutz lay for a moment with his tongue hanging out. Then he staggered over to me. I hugged him and said, "I thought you were done for that time, Klutzie."

"I thought it was a monster from another world," said the unicorn.

"He's not a monster! He's my dog, and neither of us wants to be here. We want to be there!" I waved my hand up at the blue sky. "If you were a flying horse, you could just fly us back into our living room."

"Where exactly is your … *living room*?" asked the unicorn, looking up at the sky.

"I don't know," I shouted. "We were looking down at a puzzle, and the next thing I knew we were splashing around in that silly pond."

"There's one way to go up. It's at the top of the mountain."

"What is it?" I asked hopefully.

"The tower, of course," said the unicorn, trotting off toward the forest.

Tower? I was hoping for a rocket ship. "Wait! Can I ride on your back?"

He stopped to glare back at me. "Do I look like a horse?" he snorted, and with a flick of his tail he disappeared into the dense trees.

Klutz and I scrambled after him. The trees closed in, blocking out the sunlight. I could smell damp soil and strange plants. "Where's the tower?" I called.

"On top of the mountain. It's the tallest part of the castle."

"There's a castle up there?"

"Of course."

"Just like Patty imagined," I said. "I don't suppose there's a princess living in this castle, is there?"

The unicorn's voice floated back to me in the warm air. "A princess?" Then he snorted or laughed. I wasn't sure which.

4.
JILL AND JACK!

Sweat ran down my face and dripped off my chin. Strange insects buzzed around my head. I glanced back at Klutz. He looked as hot and miserable as I felt. But the unicorn paid no attention to us. He trotted up the steep path, his long tail swishing behind him.

Suddenly the forest ended, and there stood the castle. It was a sad-looking heap of rocks with a tower at one end. But at least it was high – high enough to reach the sky.

25

"Here we are!" said the unicorn. "Now climb up the tower and be off with you."

"Where's a door?" I asked.

"Door? All the doors are locked," he said.

"How are we supposed to get inside?" I asked.

"Inside?" the unicorn laughed. "You have to climb up the outside of the tower."

I sat right down in the tall grass. "I am not climbing some dumb tower! Do you expect us to jump off the top or something?"

The unicorn pawed the grass and tossed his head. I could see he was getting angry. "It isn't my job to give you the answers! This is your adventure!"

"Look! There's somebody up there," I said.

The unicorn looked up at the small face that had appeared at the open window. "Oh, dear, she's seen me," he muttered.

"Hey, Unicorn!" called the face. "What are you doing, and who's that with you?"

"Another human," the unicorn said. "I told him he wasn't welcome here. He's trying to get back to his *living room*."

"Hello, boy!" said the princess. She sounded very cheerful for someone who was locked up in a tower.

"Who are you?" I asked grumpily. "Rapunzel, I suppose."

"No, my name is Jill, so you must be Jack. You know, Jack and Jill went up the hill."

"My name is L.B. Jones," I yelled.

"Oh, well, I think I'll call you Jack, all the same," she said.

What is it with girls? They're always trying to rename me. Klutz came over and flopped down next to me. He looked tired. He'd done more walking today than he usually does in a week.

The unicorn was looking at me with those big eyes of his. "What are you doing?" he asked.

"Resting."

"And after you've rested, you'll carry on with your adventure, right?"

That was the second time he'd said something silly about *my* adventure. "How can I carry on?" I said. "I don't have any control over what happens in this world – or my own world, it seems."

"You could try using your imagination," he said.

"I don't have any," I snapped at him.

Then Jill yelled down at me again, "What are you doing, lazy bones?"

That was the last straw. "My name is not Lazy Bones!" I yelled at her. Suddenly I knew I had to show them that I wasn't lazy. And the only way to do that was staring me in the face. The tower! I had to climb that tall and dangerous tower.

5.
THE TOWER!

I was so angry, I climbed the first twenty feet without even thinking.

"Hey! " Jill yelled down at the top of my head. "You're coming up! Great!" She sounded impressed.

But as I got higher, I began to feel dizzy. I didn't look down or up. I kept my eyes on the wall just a little above my head, searching for handholds.

Jill's voice got louder. "You're doing it! I didn't think you had it in you, Jack!"

"My name is *not* Jack!" I felt the rock under my left foot move. My heart leaped as the rock slipped out of the wall. It bounced down the side of the tower and thudded into the ground far, far below. My fingers were getting slippery with sweat.

I was so scared, I couldn't move. It was like I was stuck there with glue.

"Just a little way more, L.B. Jones," Jill said softly. "You can do it." Her words unstuck my fingers. I inched one hand up higher and felt the lower edge of the windowsill. Her fingers touched mine, guiding them to a safe handhold. Suddenly my moist hand slipped off the ledge, but Jill grabbed my arm.

"Move your feet up higher," she said. With Jill pulling, I made it over the ledge and into the tiny tower room. From way below, I heard Klutz barking happily.

Jill grinned at me. I stared at her and said, "You don't look much like a princess!" She was dressed in jeans, a baseball cap, and a T-shirt that said "Save the whales."

"There are all kinds of princesses, you know."

I shrugged. "I'm not even going to ask how you ended up in this place."

"Good! Because I don't know how it happened. Let's just get out of here!"

I looked at the round walls of the room. There was one door. The room was bare except for a small rug and some empty burger bags.

"The door has a lock way up high on the inside," said Jill. "I've been trying to reach it, but I can't. There's nothing in this room to use to poke at it. And I've been yelling at that silly unicorn every time he trots by, but he's been no help at all."

I looked at the lock, which was at least ten feet above our heads. No way could I leap that high. But my thoughts were jumping around inside my head. Suddenly I realized that even though I was scared, I was not bored. My imagination kicked in, and I could see a way to unlock the door.

"I've got an idea! A plan! But it might not work, and if the door is locked from the outside as well, we're really in trouble."

So we used my plan. I crouched down right next to the wall, Jill climbed onto my shoulders, and I stood up slowly. She was a lot heavier than she looked!

"OK," she said. "I can reach it! Now, if I can just move the bolt." I could hear her muttering to herself while her feet dug into my shoulders. "It's rusty," she said. "Wait …. There! I did it!" She jumped off my shoulders without waiting for me to crouch down. "Hurry! Let's see if it opens!"

I grabbed the doorknob and pulled. With a groan and a creak, the door swung toward us. We peered out of our prison at a narrow, winding staircase. It was completely covered in cobwebs.

"Oh, yuck! I hate spiders!" said Jill.

6.

SPIDERS AND STRAWS!

Spiders are not my favorite creatures either! But I didn't see any big, juicy ones on the webs. I looked at the trash on the floor. "Do you have a straw?" I asked.

"Sure. Two of them. I always drink with two straws."

As we stumbled down the steep stone steps, I used the straws to push the cobwebs out of the way. I could still feel a few sticky threads brush my face, and Jill kept yelling "Yuck!" every few seconds.

"I want to go home," she said as we reached the last step and entered a dark, dusty hallway.

"Where is your home?" I asked.

I wasn't surprised when she answered, "Chicago! I was just sitting in my bedroom, eating my burger and fries. I was doing this puzzle with my sister – a picture of a castle. My little sister wanted to put in the last piece, but I did it. And then, poof, there I was. In that stupid tower room."

We came to a door in the outside wall of the castle. But even when we both shoved together, we couldn't budge it.

"Let us out!" I shouted.

"Help!" yelled Jill.

We heard Klutz barking and something scraping and scratching on the outside of the door. When we pushed again, the door fell off its hinges and we toppled out into the sunshine. Klutz pounced on me and licked my face. The unicorn stood there, tossing his head to show off his horn. He had ripped off the vines that were covering the door! "Now, what's the next step?" he asked.

41

That was a good question. The tower hadn't helped us to get out of the puzzle world.

"If puzzles brought us here …" Jill said slowly.

"Maybe they can take us back!" I shouted. "Where would we find a puzzle in this place? Not in the forest. In the castle, maybe?"

We all went back in through the broken-down door. "What an unpleasant place," said the unicorn. "Where do you think these puzzles might be?"

"There's no attic … so let's look in the basement," I said, using my imagination. But my imagination didn't prepare me for the basement of the castle. It was a dungeon. We climbed down the steps into the scariest place I've ever been. It smelled terrible.

"How are we ever going to find anything down here?" whispered Jill, just as Klutz crashed into something skinny and white. A skeleton! The head rolled off and bumped against an old trunk.

After about five minutes of us screaming and Klutz barking, the unicorn used his horn to pry open the trunk. Inside, we could see lots of boxes – puzzles! I was right. Maybe I did have an imagination after all!

We dragged the puzzles out and laid them on the damp floor of the dungeon. I wasn't sure what we should be looking for. Then Jill yelled, "Hey! Here's one that shows the park by my house!"

Klutz gave an excited woof. I saw a box that showed our little white house.

"Now what?" asked Jill. She was shaking with excitement.

"I know, I'll do your puzzle and you do mine. Then we'll put each other's last piece in." It was a good plan, only Jill was a lot faster than I was at doing puzzles.

She finished and sat there, holding the last piece in front of me and saying, "Hurry up, L.B. Jones! Move it!"

When the park puzzle had just one tiny hole left in it, we handed each other our last pieces. Jill leaned toward me and whispered, "I'm going to miss you, L.B. Jones!" Then she kissed me on the cheek.

As I was saying "Why'd you go and do that!" and wiping my face, she put in the last piece of puzzle. Poof! She was gone!

The unicorn tossed his head and muttered, "One down, two to go."

Klutz whined and shoved his nose under my hand. I took a gulp of the stale, smelly air. I grabbed Klutz's paw and held it on top of the puzzle and then shoved that last piece into the picture of our house.

POOF! CRASH!

7.
IMAGINE!

I fell off the couch with Klutz on top of me. We both jumped up, shook ourselves, and looked around.

There were all the puzzles, just like we'd left them. Except the one of the waterfall. It was still missing one piece! I heard Patty trotting down the stairs, so I jumped back onto the couch.

"I can't find that missing piece anywhere," she said. "I've been up and down to the attic five times while you've been sleeping like a log."

Sleeping? I hopped up and patted my pockets. "Here it is!" I said. I pulled out the bit of blue and handed it to Patty.

"You had it all along?"

"Yeah, I guess. I hid it. I got tired of you always putting in the last piece. The next puzzle you do, I promise to help," I said.

"Well, OK," Patty said as she took the piece from me. She looked at it and asked, "You want to put this one in for me?"

"No way!" I said. Klutz agreed. He barked once and ran into the kitchen. I watched as Patty lined up the edges and pressed the bit of blue water into the pond. Nothing. I let my breath out slowly. So, had it really been a dream?

"Hey, look, L.B. The sun's out! Let's go shoot some hoops."

"Okay! I'll get my ball and meet you out there," I said.

Patty looked surprised at my answer. "Really? What's got into you?" When I shrugged, she stuck out her tongue and dashed outside.

I stared at the puzzle. A waterfall, trees, a pond, boulders, a stretch of sand. I looked at the sand. I couldn't see the message I'd scratched into it. Of course not. It had all been a dream. But wait, what was that noise? Could it be the waterfall? I leaned closer to the puzzle. No, I told myself, I just have some water in my ears. Water?

I knew you wouldn't believe me!

But, hey, do me a favor, will you? If you ever find a puzzle that shows this nice little park, let me know. I forgot to get Jill's address. I imagine that visiting her through a puzzle is the only way I'll get to see her again.